THE BEST TEACHER EVER

BY MERCER MAYER

To Grandma Kathy Skiles,
the Best Teacher Ever!

HarperFestival®

A Division of HarperCollinsPublishers

HarperCollins®, ▰®, and HarperFestival® are trademarks of HarperCollins Publishers.
Copyright © 2008 Mercer Mayer. All rights reserved. LITTLE CRITTER, MERCER MAYER'S LITTLE CRITTER and
MERCER MAYER'S LITTLE CRITTER and logo are registered trademarks of Orchard House Licensing Company. All rights reserved.
Printed in the United States of America.
For information address HarperCollins Children's Books, a division of HarperCollins Publishers, 195 Broadway, New York, NY 10007.
Library of Congress catalog card number: 2007933687
ISBN 978-0-06-053960-3
A Big Tuna Trading Company, LLC/J. R. Sansevere Book
www.harpercollinschildrens.com   www.littlecritter.com
14 15 16 17 CWM 20 19 18 17 16 15
❖
First Edition

Miss Kitty is my teacher. She is the best teacher ever! She reads stories to us at story time and makes them fun. Sometimes she puts on a silly costume.

She teaches math and makes it exciting.

Sometimes she brings special treats just for us.

We go on field trips, and we sing songs on the bus.

When we went to the zoo, she told us all about the animals. Did you know that elephants flap their ears to keep cool? I wish I could do that.

I wanted to do something special for Miss Kitty on teacher appreciation day.

I asked Dad, "But what can I do?"

I went to Dad's shop to make her something really special. Dad showed me all his tools. But using them looked too hard.

Later Mom took me to the mall. I found just the right present.

Mom said, "I don't think Miss Kitty would really like a Robot Critter-zilla."

Probably not, but I would. "Please, Mom?" I asked. "No," Mom said.

Then Mom said, "How about we bake her something?"
I liked that idea.

We drove home.

Mom made my favorite cake for Miss
Kitty. I helped.

I put my cake on the table in the front
hall so I wouldn't forget it in the morning.
I was all set for teacher appreciation day.

I woke up early and ran downstairs. But
my cake was on the floor. The dog had eaten
most of it.

"I bet Miss Kitty would love a big bouquet of flowers," said Mom.

She quickly cut a bunch from the garden. Then she wrapped a ribbon around them.

"Here you go," she said. "And hurry. The bus is almost here."

I ran out the front door with my bouquet of flowers for Miss Kitty.

On the bus everyone had big presents in big
boxes wrapped in pretty bows. My present
didn't look so good. I hid it under my seat.

I was almost to my classroom when I noticed that I forgot my flowers on the bus. The bus was leaving. *Oh, no! What am I going to do now?* I thought.

I ran to the back of the classroom.
I got out my drawing pad and drew
the quickest, best picture ever.

When it was my turn, I walked up to the front of the class. With everyone looking at me . . .

. . . I gave my picture to Miss Kitty.

She smiled. Then she put it up on her bulletin board. Mine was the only picture up there.

What a great present . . .

. . . for the best teacher ever.

the end